The Time Machine Girls

ERNESTINE TITO JONES

Jones, Ernestine Tito
The Time Machine Girls
Book Four: Teamwork
Website: www.ernestinetitojones.com

The Time Machine Girls

4

Teamwork

Chapter One

Hazel and Bess both sat on the thin pink rug in the bedroom they shared. The Lego instruction manual was opened in front of them. They had just begun building the cute Lego hospital set their grandparents bought for them when they all went into town a few days ago.

Hazel could hardly believe they'd bought it for them. Neither girl had even asked for it. And Hazel couldn't wait to play with it when she and Bess were done putting it together, even though half of the fun was usually putting it together.

It was not as much fun when you were expected to build the set with someone who didn't care about getting things right.

Hazel adjusted her perfect ponytail as she carefully sifted through Lego pieces to find the exact one they needed.

Bess picked up the wrong piece again, and shoved it into the other blocks. Hazel turned to her. "That's not the right piece, Bess," she said, tugging it off. She pointed to the picture in the instruction manual. "We're looking for a white rectangular piece with four studs, not three."

"Oh," Bess said, looking at the photo. "This one is probably close enough."

"It's not close enough. It has to be perfect, or the whole hospital will be built wrong," Hazel replied.

"Maybe I like hospitals that are built

wrong."

A steady stream of rain pattered the window outside. It was another rainy day stuck inside with her six-year-old sister.

Hazel took a deep breath and tried to calm down, but the whole room was a mess, thanks to Bess. The Lego set had come with four numbered bags of Legos. But instead of opening them one at a time, Bess had dumped all four bags onto the floor and was sitting in the middle of the pile. Her wild blonde hair hadn't been combed yet today even though their mother had told her to do it. And, she was still in her long, blue dress-up dress because she wasn't done playing movie star with her stuffed animals yet.

How was Hazel supposed to put together a Lego set with someone who thought close enough was good enough, and didn't even clean up one mess before she started another one?

Bess lifted up a pink piece with four studs. "Found it," she said.

"That's still not right. It needs to be a white piece." Hazel groaned and opened the door to their room.

"Where are you going?" Bess asked.

"Downstairs for a second," Hazel said. "I'm just feeling frustrated, and I need a minute to myself."

Taking a small break was one of the things her mother suggested Hazel do when she got upset with her little sister. Writing in a journal was another. Hazel wasn't sure either one was going to work.

She shut the door behind her, listening as the soft patter of rain fell against the roof outside. She grabbed the banister to head downstairs, but then she turned and looked at the narrow stairwell that led to the attic.

She and Bess hadn't been in the attic in days. The last time they went in there was when they took the time machine back to 1849, and the Underground Railroad. That was also the day she accidentally found a box full of photos that she wanted to look through more. Now would be a good time to do that. Her mother had told Bess that when Hazel needed a break from her that she shouldn't follow Hazel.

Thunder shook the house as Hazel stared at the stairwell. Was she really about to go into the creepy, smelly attic by herself during a thunderstorm? She wasn't even supposed to go into the attic at all. It went against the rules, and she usually tried to follow those. Hazel looked at the door to her bedroom.

Slowly, she tiptoed up the stairs to the attic.

Chapter Two

The attic was darker than usual because there wasn't much light coming in from the window. Little dripping noises from the rain reminded Hazel of a broken faucet.

Drip. Drip. Drip.

She knew she shouldn't be in here by herself. Her grandfather hadn't given her the wink to let her know it was safe to use the time machine yet. But she wasn't in here to use the time machine. She was in here to look through the box of photos.

The weird smell of musty attic mixed with old machine parts made Hazel reach for the hand sanitizer in her back pocket even though she hadn't touched anything yet.

She walked over to the back wall where she remembered the box was at the last time she was in here.

Even though the light was on, it wasn't doing much to light the attic because the sky was so dark. And she couldn't tell one box from another. She lifted one of the lids. Rusty machine parts filled the box. She lifted another. Old newspapers.

The boxes looked the same. They were all cardboard boxes with lids. On the fifth box, just when she was starting to think her grandparents had hidden it, she found it.

Black and white photos looked back at her. She didn't recognize any of the relatives in the photos. She dug down deeper into the box. Dust coated her fingertips, but she needed to find the photo from the county fair. She knew that was the day things had changed for her family. Her grandparents used to be professors at a college in the city. But, after the day at the fair when they were supposed to show the world their time machine, they moved to the farmhouse and began a quiet life of vegetable farming.

Under the black-and-white photos was a small stack of color ones. She saw one of her mother when she was about nine or ten. She was holding a humungous blue cotton candy as she smiled next to a man with a dark beard and a dark-haired woman with curls. Hazel knew those were her grandparents, even though they didn't look much like themselves in the photo.

She also knew the photo must have been from the fair.

It was strange to see how much Hazel looked like her mother when they were similar ages. Her brown hair was pulled back perfectly in braids hanging off to the side. The sign behind them said "World's First Working Time Machine," but her grandparents did not look happy. They were barely smiling, not that they smiled that much now. But they weren't happy in the photo. What happened that day?

"Hazel!" Her mother called from downstairs. "Where are you? I have something to go over with you and your sister!"

Hazel dropped the stack of photos. They scattered off to the side of the box and she scrambled to pick them up and stuff them back in.

She couldn't let her mother find out she was in here, looking for the family secret. Her mother was the last person who could know that. Before the girls left with their mother to go to the farmhouse for the summer, Hazel overheard her mother talking about a family secret she wanted to make sure the girls didn't find out about. She couldn't know Hazel was looking for clues to that secret.

Quickly, Hazel shut the box on the photos and ran out the door and down the narrow stairwell that led to the second floor then down the other set of stairs to the main level. She would have to come back to the attic later.

"Sorry, Mom," she said when she finally reached the kitchen where her mother and sister were. "I was just taking a break from Bess like you told me to when I got frustrated."

Technically, that wasn't a lie, Hazel told herself even though she still felt terrible saying it. She was an honest and responsible eight-year-old, but she was also determined to find the family secret, bring her family closer, and convince her grandparents to take the time machine with them when they moved. It was a huge goal, and she wondered if she'd be able to do it.

She sat down on a bar stool next to her sister and watched her mother write stuff on the whiteboard hanging on the wall in the kitchen. Her arms swung wildly as she wrote, but Hazel had no idea what she was writing yet.

She looked over at Bess, but Bess didn't

look back. She had her arms folded and her nose in the air.

Was she still mad about the Legos?

Bess smiled at Froggenstein, her pet frog, who was sitting in a plastic aquarium on the kitchen counter in front of her, then turned to Hazel and stuck her tongue out. "You left me with a big Lego mess," she finally said.

"You made the big Lego mess," Hazel replied. "It's part of the reason I had to leave. I was getting frustrated."

"But you said you were going downstairs," Bess said, even louder. "And then you went into the attic."

Hazel watched her mother's reaction when Bess said that.

The black marker smeared across the whiteboard. Their mother stopped writing and turned toward the girls. "What did you say, Bess? Where were you at, Hazel?"

Chapter Three

Hazel gulped. She didn't know Bess had seen her go into the attic. And she didn't know what to say. She stumbled over her words. "I...I..."

"I was just kidding," Bess said. "Hazel would never do that. She's the responsible one. I just didn't see her when I went downstairs. But, I'm sure she was in the bathroom or something."

Their mother shook her head and went back to her whiteboard.

Hazel smiled at her sister, but Bess didn't smile back.

The smell of bacon and eggs still filled

the kitchen. And Hazel's stomach ached thinking about how much she'd eaten that morning. She was getting used to her grandmother's home-cooked meals. She was getting used to a lot of things around her grandparents' boring farmhouse. Even without internet or TV, it almost didn't seem boring anymore, and it wasn't just because of the time machine.

Her mother hummed as she erased and added things with the thick black marker she was holding, but Hazel didn't recognize the song she was humming.

"There," she said, stepping back to admire her list. She turned around to face the girls. "That ought to keep you busy for a while."

Hazel couldn't believe it. It was a chore list, and there were ten things on it.

"It's probably going to be rainy all day," she said, kissing the girls on the top of their heads. "So since you're stuck inside anyway, you might as well make the best of it and get some stuff done."

The girls both groaned.

"Oh stop," their mother said. "It's not all chores. I added something fun there at the end. But only if you get your chores done."

Bess finally stopped turning and looked up. "Number one. C-c-lee-ann."

"Good job, Bess," their mother said, encouragingly. "You're doing such a great job with your reading. That says 'clean.' Clean up your room."

Bess repeated the words back. She was about to enter first grade, and she still had to sound out most words.

"That list is going to take forever," Hazel complained, mostly because she knew who was actually going to be the one doing most of the work. She also knew who was actually the one who had messed up the room in the first place. Their room was only half-messy, and it wasn't Hazel's half.

"It won't take forever if you work together and make a plan for getting it done," their mother replied cheerfully.

Their mother was a teacher and this sounded a lot like one of her "teaching moments" to Hazel.

Hazel wondered how she was going to help her mom teach Bess to follow a plan or work together. That girl was a walking disaster.

Bess stopped spinning her barstool. "Good idea, Mom. We need to work together. I don't want to get stuck cleaning Hazel's messes again, like usual."

Hazel rolled her eyes. Was her sister serious? Nothing could have been further from the truth.

"Now remember, Hazel's in charge," their mother said as she walked out to the hall.

"Froggenstein and I can't believe you went into the attic without me," Bess yelled. "You made me promise I wouldn't go in there alone, and then you went in there."

Hazel gulped and shushed her sister in case their mother could hear her from the other room. "Honestly, Bess. Why are you always so loud? Mom is going to hear." She lowered her voice. "We'll talk about this later."

Bess hopped off the barstool and walked closer to the whiteboard mounted to the wall in the kitchen. "Number ten..." she said. "Play da-tee with Bob...bee?"

Hazel looked up so fast her neck hurt. *What was her sister trying to read?*

Her face dropped. There in bold black letters with a smiley face next to it read...

10) Enjoy a play date with Bobby.

Was their mother kidding? Not again!

Chapter Four

The back door opened, and their
grandfather came in, stomping and
shuffling his wet boots onto the brown
straw mat at the back of the kitchen.
Shaking his umbrella out into the rain, he
turned toward the girls. Hazel and Bess
both ran over to him, and gave him a big
hug before he could even shut the door.

"Who's up for an adventure today?" he
said while he laughed into the girls' hugs.
His thick shaggy eyebrows covered most of
his eyes and his beard covered most of his
smile, so he always looked angry no matter
how he was really feeling. Hazel was only

beginning to realize he wasn't as grumpy as he looked.

Bess pointed up to the whiteboard on the wall, pouting. "Before we can go anywhere fun, we have to finish the million gazillion things on our to-do list."

Their grandfather mumbled to himself as he read the items on the whiteboard. "Hmmm, clean room, dust the living room... this shouldn't take you very long." His shaggy eyebrows rose when he got to the last item, though. "I see your biggest problem is going to be number ten," he said, taking off his raincoat.

"What are we going to do?" Hazel said. "We'll never be able to use the time machine today!"

"The w-w-what?" their mother stammered as she returned to the kitchen.

She was carrying an umbrella and boots, but she dropped them both when Hazel said "time machine." They fell onto the floor by her feet.

Bess elbowed Hazel. "Now who's the loud one?" she said under her breath. "Or the one who doesn't follow the rules..."

Grandpa winked at Hazel and Bess. "The girls were telling me about a game they'd like to play. But they're worried they won't be able to play it if they have to have a play date with Bobby."

"Nonsense. It'll probably make the game even more fun to have another person playing, whatever the game is," their mother said, looking proudly at her list.

Their grandfather rolled up his sleeves and mumbled something under his breath as he left the room.

Their mother didn't seem to notice. "Bobby's mom told me he talks about nothing else but playing here again. Isn't that nice? He was really sorry about what happened last time..."

Hazel stopped herself from rolling her eyes. Bobby's mother and Hazel's mother grew up together, so they liked each other. But, the last time he came over, he tried to steal Bess's frog. He said she was too young to take care of it so she should just give it to him. And when Bess and Hazel tried to get away from him, he followed them into the attic, and saw them leaving in the time machine. Bobby became very curious about the time machine after that. And he was determined to catch the girls using it.

Hazel knew Bobby didn't really want to

have a play date. He just wanted to snoop around so he could learn more about the time machine and their family secret, something Hazel wanted to do too, just not with Bobby. But she couldn't tell any of this to her mom.

Their mother went on. "I tried to tell him it was going to be rainy all day so you kids wouldn't be able to play outside at all. Strangely, he seemed even more eager to come over."

Bess's eyes grew extra large behind her thick glasses as everything finally sunk in. "So if we do all the chores on this list," she asked, "the fun thing we get to do is have a play date with Bobby?" She scrunched her face like she'd bitten into a lemon. "No thank you."

"Bess, I'd like a better attitude," their

mother replied. "Bobby said he was sorry. Let's give him another chance, okay?"

Their mother put her boots on as she spoke. "I told him you girls would probably be finishing up your to-do list around lunch, so he could come over for a couple hours in the afternoon."

Bess grabbed Froggenstein's aquarium from off the counter. "Well then, I guess we'd better get going on that list," she said.

Hazel couldn't believe her sister really said that. *Was she up to something?*

"That's the spirit," their mother replied, zipping up a boot. "If only it were that easy to get your grandparents on a good schedule." She grabbed her umbrella. It shook nervously in her hand as she looked out the window at the rain. "I... I thought we'd be tackling the attic by now. But we're still on the barn. It's almost like they're stalling..."

She seemed to snap out of it, opening the door. A whoosh of wind blew her curls across her face. "We'd better tackle that soon." She looked around. "Where's your grandfather? No wonder we can't get anything done."

She yelled over her shoulder as she opened the umbrella into the rain. "Come on, Dad! Mom's waiting in the barn."

"I'll meet you in there," their grandfather called from the other room.

Their mother turned before she left into the rain. "There are sandwiches in the fridge if you get hungry. I'll be in the barn if you need me. And remember to listen for Bobby this afternoon."

As soon as the door closed behind her,

their grandfather came back into the room.

"You heard your mother," he said, walking over to the girls. "Your grandmother and I will stall as long as we can, but we're going to have to get to that attic soon. So, we need to hurry up and return things to history."

"Why?" Bess asked.

"We won't be able to take the time machine with us when we leave. And your mother can't know it's even here," their grandfather said. Hazel wondered how they were going to hide it from her when they cleaned out the attic.

He held out a closed fist. "That's why I'm giving you both this," he said.

Chapter Five

Her grandfather opened his hand. He was holding a small key. "I was going to pick something for you to return, but I didn't have time," he said. "Your mother is in a rush to move us off the farm."

"Why is she in such a rush?" Bess asked.

Their grandfather held the key out, and Hazel took it.

"I don't think she likes it here," he said. "She's ready to get back to her old life and forget about... things again."

Bess hugged their grandpa. "That's not true," she said.

Their grandfather grabbed his raincoat from the coat hanger by the back door where it was drying and put it back on. "At any rate, that's the key to the trunk. Pick something to return."

Hazel's eyes widened. She looked around to make sure her mother couldn't hear her even though she'd already left. "How are we supposed to go in the time machine when we have to play with Bobby this afternoon?"

"Work together. I'm sure you'll figure it out."

"Work together?" Bess groaned. "Why is everyone always telling us to do that? Have you seen the Legos in our room? We're not very good at it."

Hazel shot her sister a look. She was the one who wasn't very good at working together.

Their grandfather smiled. "I'm sure you'll both do just fine. I've got to go."

He turned back around before he left. "Choose anything you want from the things in the trunk, but if you pick the crank, don't go inside the main laboratory. In fact, make sure that door just stays closed. It's dangerous. And if you pick the glasses, be sure to tell everyone you're returning them for your grandfather."

Hazel had no idea what any of that meant, but she nodded as her grandfather winked and shuffled out onto the back porch

"One more thing," he said, poking his head back in as he opened his umbrella. "We've never talked about this before, but it's probably the most important thing.

Whatever you do, be careful not to change history. You cannot leave anything from the future behind when you leave or take anything from the past with you..."

"But you took stuff, Grandpa," Bess said, interrupting.

"Yes, and that was a mistake." Their grandfather looked out into the rain. "Just be careful what you do while you're there or you could change history," he said as he shut the door.

After their grandfather left, Hazel tried to remember all the warnings he'd just given them, but she'd been so worried about Bobby and having the key to the trunk that she hadn't remembered a thing. She decided she would just make sure they didn't choose the glasses or the crank from the trunk. That way, they wouldn't have to worry about remembering warnings.

But one warning stuck out more than anything else.

Hazel looked at her sister, who was now spinning around the room, pretending to be princess dancing with her frog. She stumbled into the bar stool and almost fell over.

"How am I going to keep Bess from changing history?" she wondered.

Chapter Six

Up in their room, Bess took Froggenstein out of his carrier and plopped herself down on her unmade bed next to a balled-up blanket. "Here's my plan," she said as she hugged her frog. "Let's leave now. Then when we get back, we'll hurry up and clean everything up. Mom will never know. Good plan, huh?"

Hazel shook her head. It was a good plan, but it went against all the rules. "You heard Mom. We need to clean first," she said, pulling out her old tattletale notebook and a pencil from one of her dresser drawers.

"Are you going to tell on me?" Bess asked.

"No. I'm making a plan to clean the room." Hazel looked around. "Let's see, the dolls, Legos, crayons, pipe cleaners, and globs of string are all your mess, not to mention the book castle you made in the corner and the stuffed-animal audience for the show you put on earlier. So, clean all of that up, and I'll dust."

Bess scrunched her face. "Mom said to work together. And you're giving me all the hard jobs," she said. "That's not fair."

"It's fair because you made the hard jobs. I'm only asking you to clean up your own mess."

Bess got up and placed Froggenstein into the middle of the book castle she'd made in the corner. Hazel grimaced at all the frog germs being smeared all over her sister's side of the room. How were they so different? Her sister was messy and never followed the rules.

She pulled the bottle of hand sanitizer from the back pocket of her jeans and squirted some into the palms of her hands.

"Okay, there's only one fair way to settle this." Bess picked up a coin from off the floor and flipped it into the air. "Heads, we do my plan. Tails, we never ever do yours."

Bess laughed so hard she coughed on her own spit.

Rrrrrrrrrribbbbbet.

"You're right, Froggenstein," Bess said, nodding to her frog like she could actually understand him. "My plan is better."

"Bess, I'm just following the rules."

"What rule were you following when

you went up to the attic earlier without me?" she asked. "I should tell Mom about it."

Hazel gasped. She dropped her pencil onto her bed. She'd forgotten that her sister had seen her go up there and that she hadn't said anything to their mom.

Hazel stood up and walked over to her sister's bed. She grabbed the blanket and started straightening her sheets. "I'll help you clean up, but we need to follow the plan and do that first." Hazel tucked in Bess's blanket and picked up some of her stuffed animals. Hazel wasn't sure if she should tell Bess about the clues she'd been finding in the attic. She decided not to. "It was wrong for me to go into the attic. I should've asked Grandpa first before I went up there..."

"And," Bess said. "You should've included me. You never include me in your plans, unless it's the plan that I should clean up everything."

"So far, you're not cleaning up anything." Hazel looked around. "I'll put the Legos back in their bags too."

Bess didn't move from her spot on the floor with her frog. She crossed her arms and stared at the ceiling.

"You're right. I'm sorry. I'll include you next time," Hazel said, pulling the key from out of her pocket. She ran a finger along its jagged edge, thinking about what item she'd choose to return to history. "So, what do you think Grandpa meant by a crank?" she asked, unsure of what a crank was. She didn't want to accidentally pick it. She looked up. Bess had already put

Froggenstein back in his carrier.

"Good idea," Bess replied, pointing to the key in Hazel's hand. Grabbing Hazel's arm, she tugged her sister across the room and out to the hall. Hazel's tennis shoes crunched over the Legos. "I see you've got the key out. That means we both agree. My plan is better. We'll clean when we get back. It's the only way we'll be able to do everything."

Hazel shook her head. "I didn't bring the key out because I thought we should change the plan." She yanked her hand free from her sister's grasp. "Mom says we have to finish our chores first. And that's that." She was the one in charge, so she was going to make sure Bess followed her plan for once.

Bess took off running, right about the

time Hazel realized her hand was empty. She was no longer holding the key, and Bess was already halfway up the stairs to the attic.

Chapter Seven

"Wait for me!" Hazel yelled as she ran up the stairs after her sister. The staircase was especially cold and dark because of the rain. The damp smell of must surrounded her.

Why didn't Bess ever follow the rules or the plans?

But Bess's plan was better, Hazel hated to admit it. The only thing they knew was that Bobby was coming over after lunch, and they wouldn't be able to use the time machine after he came over.

The attic door creaked open and Hazel blinked her eyes, trying to force them to adjust to the dim lighting of the attic. She looked around for the bookcase, the time machine, and the trunk.

The sound of thunder rattled the window as the storm picked up again.

"Bess," she called into the shadows of the attic. "Where are you? Don't pick something without me. We're supposed to work together."

Even though Hazel was just in the attic alone, it seemed creepier and darker now that the storm was picking up and the sky was a darker gray. The attic always smelled funny, but especially funny whenever it rained.

Hazel scanned the floorboards and dark corners where boxes full of overflowing machine parts were stacked along the sides. She thought about her grandparents, and how they were stalling because they didn't want to clean out the attic. She wondered if they really wanted to move from the farmhouse at all. Maybe, they were just being forced to follow someone else's plan.

Hazel's eyes stopped on a shiny blue dress and sneakers. Just as she suspected, Bess was sitting in front of the open trunk, pulling things out one after another.

"There's not much in here," she said, barely looking up from the mess in front of her. There always seemed to be a mess in front of her. There was an antique wheel, a metal bar, a pair of glasses, what looked like some rope... She was spreading everything out along the sides of the army trunk faster than Hazel could watch her.

"I've made my decision," Bess said, triumphantly holding up the glasses.

"Well, thank you for including me," Hazel said, sarcastically. "But, you can't pick the glasses, Bess."

"Why? These glasses are amazing!" She took off her own thick glasses and put the thin wired ones on, then squinted and blinked wildly.

Hazel tapped her foot. "Remember? Those glasses come with weird instructions, so unless you want to follow weird instructions, pick something else. No glasses and no crank, whatever that is."

Hazel turned away, watching as her sister picked up an old glove and inspected it from every angle.

"Boring," she said, tossing the glove back into the trunk.

Hazel thought about the box of photos and the clues to the family secret. Maybe she could look through the box again while her sister looked through the items in the trunk.

"And we're only going to choose the item now. We're not going in the time machine until our chores are finished like Mom said." Hazel yelled to her sister as she walked toward the box she knew had the pictures, leaving Bess to look through the stuff in the trunk by herself.

"That should keep her busy long enough for me to look around," Hazel thought. She hoped Bess didn't really think she was going to get to pick the item by herself. They had to agree on it.

She lifted the lid to the photos and sat down beside the box. The more she thought about that box of photos and the fair, the more Hazel knew that had to be the family secret. Something happened that day that changed the family forever and she was going to find out what it was.

She pulled out a stack of photos, noticing a small notebook just underneath them. It was similar to her tattletale notebook only slightly smaller and the cover was a nice faded leather material. She picked it up and flipped to the middle of the book. The paper was yellowing like paper does when it gets old. There was a drawing of a wheelchair sitting under a domed lid. She turned to another page. Math equations. Some were crossed out, some were circled.

The notebook must have belonged to her grandparents.

Ding Dong...

Ding Dong...

Ding Dong...

The doorbell rang three times in a row. Rain poured outside the attic window.

"Do you think," Hazel said, stuffing the notebook in her back pocket so she could look through it later, "that Bobby's early?"

"Don't answer it," Bess said. "Let's just go."

Chapter Eight

Ding Dong...

Ding Dong...

Ding Dong...

Hazel ran down the narrow stairwell that led from the attic to the second set of stairs. Someone was yelling on the other side of the front door. "Open up! Or I'm telling your mom to look for you! I know she's in the barn. She's always in the barn."

The doorbell rang again and again.

It was Bobby, all right! He was early!

Bess was right behind her. She tugged on Hazel's arm. "Come on, Hazel. Let's just go in the time machine."

Hazel looked down at her tennis shoes. Nothing was going according to plan, and she wasn't sure what was the right thing to do.

She took a deep breath and looked at her sister. "We can't leave in the time machine, Bess. He said he'll tell Mom to look for us if we don't answer the door. And, if she came in and didn't see us, then we'd be in trouble. Or worse, we'd have to explain we went in the time machine."

Bess let go of Hazel's arm and both girls walked to the front door.

Ding Dong...

Hazel peeked through the peephole even though she knew who it was. Sure enough, a red-haired boy with freckles and a soggy raincoat was standing on the porch of the farmhouse. She opened the door.

"Oh good. You're here," Bobby said, looking around, practically barging his way in. "I thought you may have left in your time machine again."

Bess elbowed Hazel. "I told you we should have."

Hazel shushed her.

The red-haired boy continued. "That's right. I know all about it." He pointed at Bess then at Hazel. "Last time I was here, your little sister told me you had a time machine, but I thought she was just a little kid with a crazy imagination. Then, I saw you both disappear in some weird plastic-covered wheelchair thing, and I started to think... I bet that really was a time machine."

"We don't know what you're talking about," Hazel said. She turned to close the door. "Sorry, Bobby. We're busy with chores. We'll probably be busy all day."

When Hazel's back was turned to him, Bobby yanked the notebook from Hazel's back pocket.

"What's this?" he asked.

"Give that back. It's none of your business."

He opened it up...

Bobby's face twisted into confusion as he stared at the page. "What is this? Your secret drawings?"

Just then a large woman with glasses came up behind him, carrying an umbrella. It was Bobby's mom. "There you are, Bobby. Let the girls finish their chores. You can come back this afternoon." She turned to the girls. "I'm so glad your mom agreed to a play date. He just can't wait to hang out with you two."

Hazel grabbed the notebook back from Bobby and watched as they walked off the porch and into the rain.

"Do we really have to have a play date with Bobby?" Bess asked when they left.

Hazel couldn't shut the door fast enough. "I don't think there's any way we can get out of it," she said. "Because moms are involved. When moms make the plans, it's a done deal. But there's one thing I do know."

"What?" asked Bess.

"We're going in that time machine right now. And we need to hurry." Hazel grabbed her sister by the arm and they rushed up the stairs.

Bess grinned as she yelled. "See? I told you my plan was better."

"It was," Hazel said. "But you have to promise to clean when we get back."

"I'll be so fast," Bess agreed. She pointed to Hazel's back pocket as they climbed the stairs again. "What was that notebook, anyway?"

Hazel stopped just outside their bedroom door. Bess stopped too. "I found the notebook in the attic, but I have no idea what it is. We'll have to look through it later. There's no time now. Grab Froggenstein, change into regular clothes, and let's go!"

Hazel could hardly believe she said to grab a frog, but she knew there was no way her sister was going to leave without him. They were the Time Machine Girls, and frog, after all.

As soon as Bess ran into the room to get

her frog, Hazel opened the notebook again, just in case it had something terrible in it that Bess couldn't see.

Chapter Nine

Rain hitting the roof was the only thing
Hazel could hear over her own breath as
she flipped through the yellowed, flimsy
pages of the notebook, wondering if it was a
diary, and if so, whose?

She quickly scanned the pages, which
didn't look like a diary at all, unless it was
the weirdest diary in the world. Most of the
pages had odd drawings on them. Some
that looked like the time machine taken
apart, others that looked like regular
objects like an ax or a pair of shoes. There
were also special notes written in scribbled
cursive that Hazel couldn't read because

she couldn't read cursive very well yet. But something looked like it said "It all starts at the county fair."

It all starts? She thought it all had ended.

Was this a clue to the family secret?

She stuffed the notebook back in her pocket next to the hand sanitizer when she heard Bess coming with her frog. She gave Hazel a thumbs up and a huge grin. Hazel could tell her sister was excited. Hazel was excited too.

Hazel pointed to her sister's outfit. She was still wearing the same sparkly long dress she'd been wearing before, only now she'd added a bright red, superhero cape that was tied around her neck, and a sparkly purse.

Hazel had told her sister to change into

regular clothes. How did Bess think that meant adding a cape and a purse?

"I thought you were changing into regular clothes," Hazel said.

"These are my regular clothes," Bess explained.

Hazel rolled her eyes. "Last time you were freezing in your fairy costume. I don't think you're going to be comfortable in that, and I don't want to hear you complaining." Hazel hated being the practical one all the time.

Bess untied the red cape and threw it into the room on top of the Lego mess. "Much better. Let's go," she said.

They ran giggling up the stairs and into the attic. "Okay, are you ready to choose something?" Hazel asked.

"I already did," Bess replied, pulling the

pair of glasses from her huge sparkly purse.

Weird shadows bounced across the walls as Hazel walked through the dark attic to the messy pile of stuff in front of the old army trunk. She put everything back in the trunk and grabbed a black, crooked, metal bar from off the top that was about the size of her arm. "We talked about this, Bess. Put the glasses back," she said as she pulled the blanket off the time machine hidden in the corner and got in. "We need to make sure we don't pick anything that comes with special instructions because I don't remember what Grandpa said. Do you?"

Bess shook her head no.

"So, we don't want to pick anything that seems like it's going to be complicated. We'll take the glasses back next time. Let's just grab this simple metal bar, return it, and come home fast so we can clean up."

"Why do you get to decide what to pick? We were supposed to work together," Bess said. She crossed her arms and threw her nose in the air. She was upset again.

Hazel was getting frustrated, but there was no time to take a break from her sister. "You got to pick the plan," Hazel said. "I wanted to clean first, remember? So, since you got to pick the plan, I should get to pick the item. That's working together."

To her surprise, Bess agreed. She climbed in next to Hazel and helped her put part of the metal bar in the compartment under the control panel. Then she strapped them both in. "My plan was better," she said.

They pushed the green button together

and the time machine chugged into its familiar rumbling. Their seat bounced along with the whole attic.

Hazel looked over at her sister and smiled. Bess smiled back as she shook with the rumbling of the engine. She didn't at all seem upset that she hadn't gotten to choose the item. Maybe Bess was actually learning how to work together. Hazel put her hand on her sister's shoulder and pulled her in for a hug. Then she pushed the "go" button. No turning back now.

A light flashed. Blip. They were gone.

Chapter Ten

Hazel opened her eyes and looked around. Like always, the time machine had landed in some bushes, but this time, the bushes were along the side of a strange-looking street made of large stones. Bess was already out, yanking on Hazel's hand, trying to get her to come out too.

"Come on!" she said, tugging. "It's amazing. You have to see."

Hazel grabbed the metal bar from the time machine's compartment, got out, and looked around. It was amazing. Large buildings surrounded them with intricate patterns of animals and designs carved into their sides. Huge windows that seemed taller than their dad stretched up the buildings. Pink blossoms on some of the trees lined part of the street, making Hazel know it must have been spring.

They were in a big city, all right, but where? The more Hazel thought about it, the more it seemed pretty quiet and empty for a big city. Nobody was around.

A group of women finally approached in long, stiff dresses with long sleeves. Wide hats covered most of their faces, and they didn't seem to notice the girls at all. They nodded to an older couple as they approached them.

"What do we do?" Bess asked. "How do we know whose metal bar this is?"

Hazel hadn't thought about that one. She tried to think of a plan really fast.

"I knew that metal bar was boring," Bess said. "We should just drop it and leave."

Hazel eyed her sister suspiciously. "Drop it and leave? You were so excited to use the time machine, and now you want to go back? So we can clean our room and play something with Bobby?"

Hazel kicked her shoe into one of the stones on the road, watching the men in hats and women in long dresses laughing and chatting in front of them.

"Here's the plan," Hazel said to Bess. "We need to get their attention so we can find out whose metal bar this is. They might know."

A warm wind blew by them as Hazel tried to listen to the people talking so she could find a place to interrupt them. But when she listened, she realized she had no idea what they were saying. They were speaking a different language.

Hazel smiled and coughed. "Excuse me. Do any of you speak English," she asked. The people looked at Bess's sparkly blue outfit and Hazel's jeans and went back to talking in their different language. Hazel guessed it was probably French.

"We need to hurry up," Bess said.

"Rrrrribbbett," went her sparkly purse.

"See? Even Froggenstein agrees." Bess said, pulling the metal bar from Hazel's grasp.

She walked toward the group of people as she lifted the bar out in front of her as far as she could. "Hello. Excuse me. Anyone recognize this?" She yelled, shaking the crooked, metal bar at the couple and the group of ladies. One of the women screamed like Bess was going to hurt them. They all stared at her, then hurried down the street faster, mumbling in French.

"Bess," Hazel said. "Stop it. I think they're afraid you're going to hit them with that?"

"Really?" Bess said, twisting her face up like she hadn't thought of that. She put the bar down but kept yelling. "I'm not going to hurt you! I just want to know if anyone needs this metal bar. Did you lose it?" she said even louder than before. "Maybe somebody famous? Is anyone here famous?"

There were very few people around, but they all looked at Bess like she was crazy.

Hazel shook her head at her sister. Her sister sure seemed in a hurry to figure this out.

The ground rumbled a little under their feet and the smell of exhaust filled the air as a car sped by. It was the kind of car Hazel only saw in parades when the antique cars would come around.

This one didn't look like it was done being made, though. It didn't have a top or a windshield. The driver was wearing a thin strange hat and what looked like swimming goggles. She honked her horn at the girls.

Ah-ooo-ga!

"What year do you think this is?" Hazel asked as the car passed, shooting a cold wind up around their faces, making them cough on the smell of exhaust. "That is a very old car."

Hazel watched it leave, squinting through the bright sun, suddenly noticing something familiar off in the distance. "Bess," she said, pointing to a tall pointy metal structure she instantly recognized.

"Whoa," Bess said when she saw it. "The Waffle Tower."

"Eiffel," corrected Hazel. "The Eiffel Tower. That means we're in France. We're in Paris, France!"

Hazel grabbed her sister's hands and they both swung happily around, again and again. "I've never been out of the country before," she said. "This is the best day of my life."

"Is it?" called a woman's voice from behind them. "I'm glad someone's enjoying themselves during this horrible war. Think about the soldiers. Are they enjoying themselves?"

Hazel turned around. She was happy to

hear someone speaking in English. A group of about 20 women were approaching them fast. Most were in long white dresses with matching small white hats. But the one talking to them was in a long black dress with a collar that practically went all the way up her neck. Her hair was grayish brown and was pinned in a messy bun with strands of hair falling out everywhere. Hazel ran a hand over her own hair. Her bun was still perfect, thank goodness.

"She looks angrier than Grandpa," Bess whispered to Hazel when the woman got to them. "I told you we should have taken the glasses."

The woman held out her hand. "I believe that belongs to me, thank you," she said, motioning toward the metal bar that Bess was still holding. "I've been looking all over for it. This isn't a toy. I am about to train these ladies on how to use the x-ray cars for the war, and driving the car will be impossible if we cannot start it."

Bess handed the crooked bar over to the woman. "You start a car with a piece of metal? Where we come from, we just use a key."

The woman put her hands on her hips. "Do you mind telling me just where it is that you come from? And how on earth you came to possess this crank?"

Hazel stumbled back when she heard those words. *Oh no! Not the crank!* She'd tried so hard to avoid that one. She wracked her brain.

What had her grandfather said about the crank again?

Ernestine Tito Jones

Chapter Eleven

Hazel didn't know what to say. Bess handed over the crank and the woman tapped her thin black boot against the stone road, waiting for the girls to answer her questions.

An afternoon breeze had picked up around them, smacking Hazel's cheeks as she stood.

"I heard you yelling," the woman continued. "You said the crank must belong to someone famous. How could you have known that?"

Bess pulled her lips to the side of her face like she always did when she was thinking. "So you're famous. Who are you?"

"Please do not answer a question with a question," the woman said. "Who are you? Where are your parents? And why do you have my crank?"

"I'm Hazel and this is my sister, Bess," Hazel said, her voice shaking just a little. "We're not from around here. We found this piece of metal, but we didn't know it was yours. We didn't even know it was a crank." Hazel took a deep breath. She hadn't even needed to lie that time.

"But we're from the future," Bess explained. "So, we'd like to know what year it is and who are you because our time machine never tells us that."

Fallen pink blossoms blew by Hazel's feet as she swayed nervously along the side of the road. She could hardly believe her sister just said that.

"From the future, eh?" the woman said. "I don't have time for children's games. If you won't tell me the truth, then so be it. There is a war going on and we have lots to do." She turned around and motioned for the group to follow her. The ladies in white tried to keep up with the older lady as she made her way over to a car that was parked on the side of the large building in front of them. It was a long antique car that looked more like a van. A red cross had been painted on the side of it, and a hospital bed and some hospital equipment had been set up beside the bed.

"Looks like we're done," Bess said to Hazel. "We returned the stick. Now, let's go."

"We don't even know who she is yet,"

Hazel said. She ran to catch up to the group. Bess groaned and ran after her.

One of the younger women in white stayed behind with Hazel and Bess. "I heard your question back there. Are you really from the future?"

Bess nodded while Hazel said, "Of course not."

The young woman giggled. "Well, it's 1916," she said, leaning down so the girls could hear her. "And, of course, you know Madame Curie."

Bess shook her head. "Nope."

The woman's face fell. "Marie Curie? Don't tell me you've never heard of her. She's very famous. She was the first woman to win a Nobel prize. And, she has not one, but two of those."

"What's a Nobel Prize?" Bess asked. "I

won a prize at the carnival once. A stuffed animal. It was a lot smaller than I thought it'd be.",

Hazel hushed her sister. "I'm not sure what a Nobel Prize is exactly, but I know it's one of the best prizes a person can get in their life. It's not like a prize at a fair. You win a Nobel Prize for discovering or creating something that helps the world."

"What did she do?" Bess asked.

The woman ran a hand through her blonde hair, fixing her already perfect bun. "Madame Curie is a scientist. She's made huge discoveries in radiation."

"What's radiation?" Bess asked.

"It's a type of energy that can be used to help fight cancer or in x-ray machines." She pointed to the large building in front of them. "This is the new Radium Institute the university built just for her. But, of course, now that the war is going on, she hasn't even been able to teach here."

"Wow," Bess said, actually looking interested now. "She must be famous."

"The war has changed everything in Paris, including Madame. She's turned her skills toward saving as many soldiers as she can. She is always trying to help people. Come with us. You have to see the mobile x-ray cars she's designed. She's been driving them right up to battles. And that's what we'll be doing too. All the ladies you see in white dresses, like me, are being trained to help the soldiers in battle. X-ray machines take pictures of the inside of your body, so they can show doctors on the battlefield broken bones or where bullets are. They need people to run the machines.

And Madame is training us to do it. Teamwork."

Hazel and Bess followed the woman to the car with the cross on it where the others were already gathered around.

"Did she make the x-ray machine?" Bess asked.

The woman laughed. "No, but her knowledge in radiation is perfect to help because, like I said, x-ray machines use radiation to work. Radiation is very harmful if you don't know how to use it properly. That's why we are all learning the right way."

At the moment, Madame Curie was standing at the front of the car. The crank Bess and Hazel gave her had been placed in a hole above the bumper and just below the headlights. Madame Curie yelled out to the women around her. "In order to start the car, you must prime the engine first then turn the crank," she said. She turned the crank and the engine began to rumble loudly. It sputtered and chugged, not at all like the way cars sounded nowadays. "It's simple," Madame Curie said, sliding into the driver's seat and turning the car off.

"That's not how you start a car in the future," Bess said to the woman next to them. "My mom just pushes the on button."

"I can hardly wait for that," the woman said. Hazel knew she did not believe her sister, which was a good thing. Her sister should not have been talking about the future. The woman pointed to the dark-haired teenage girl standing next to Madame Curie. "That girl is Madame's older daughter, Irene. Everyone says she's as smart as her mother," she said.

Madame Curie motioned to the x-ray equipment in front of them. "Irene will show you all everything you need to know to work the x-ray equipment. I have to grab something from my lab."

She walked over to the girls and stopped just in front of them. "Both of you, come with me to the laboratory. I have something to discuss with you."

Hazel gulped. She remembered what her grandfather said now. "*If you pick the crank, just don't go inside the main laboratory. It's dangerous.*"

Why hadn't she let Bess pick the glasses? Maybe she was the one who wasn't good at working together, after all.

Chapter Twelve

Hazel's heart pounded inside her t-shirt as she tried to keep up with Madame Curie and Bess while everyone else in the group stayed behind to learn how to use the x-ray equipment.

Hazel had a feeling they should just have stayed behind too. The wind whooshed around Hazel's face from the warm spring breeze, making her nose itch and her eyes water a little. Bess ran in front with Marie Curie, both their long dresses gleamed in the sunshine, and Hazel had to jog to catch up. Grabbing her sister's arm, Hazel pulled her back. "We can't go in the lab, remember? Grandpa said it's dangerous."

Bess scrunched her face like she was thinking. "I don't think Madame Curie would take us someplace dangerous. She has two noodle prizes."

Hazel whispered in her sister's ear. "Nobel Prizes," Hazel corrected her sister. "And, I don't know. Maybe she doesn't know how dangerous it is yet."

"Let me think this over." Bess put her hand on her chin and pushed her lips together harder. She stared up at the sky and turned her head this way and that. "Hmmmm," she said.

Hazel rolled her eyes. "Stop pretending to think this over. We're not going in the lab."

"I'm not pretending. I'm really

thinking!" Bess shot back. "And the only thing I'm thinking is why do you always get to decide what we do?"

"Rrrrrrriiiiibbbet," went the frog in Bess's sparkly purse.

"See? Even Froggenstein agrees," she said, turning back around. She walked faster again, trying to catch up to Madame Curie.

Once again, Hazel jogged to keep up with her sister. She whispered in her ear. "Do you really think our grandfather would tell us something was dangerous if it wasn't?"

Madame Curie walked up the stairs of the large building in front of them. Thick columns, wider than a person and much, much taller stood out in front like guards. Madame Curie opened the gigantic wooden door, and as soon as Hazel stepped inside, the smell of spring blossoms turned to a chemical smell that reminded her of a hospital.

The building seemed completely empty and the only sound they heard was their own footsteps and breath as they walked up the staircase to the second floor.

"It's not usually this quiet," the scientist said, her voice echoing off the empty walls. "Most people are off fighting the war. I'm afraid it's involved most of the world."

Hazel thought about it. It must have been the first World War.

Once at the top, they walked down a long hallway, finally reaching a door. Madame Curie swung it open and motioned for the girls to step inside with her. Hazel gasped. "Is th-this your main lab?" she asked, unsure if she should go any farther.

Madame Curie smiled. "I'm glad to see you're so eager. But no, not yet. The main lab is just through the next room. Come, come," she said, hurrying the girls into the room.

Hazel looked around at the large room in front of her. There were many long, wooden tables, cluttered with papers and gadgets. None had any room to put anything else on them. They were full of strange contraptions, notebooks, and glass containers. Some of the machines were long and metal with many wires around them. Others looked like large funnels. One looked like an upside down stool. It was all very strange.

"You look afraid," she said. "Nothing in

life is to be feared. It is only to be understood, which is why I wanted to talk to you. I remember you now. I met you three years ago on a hike in the Swiss Alps." She pointed to Bess. "You look exactly the same, as if you haven't aged a day. I remember your sparkly dress the most. You were dressed just like you are now with the same purse and a frog inside it..."

Bess and Hazel both shook their heads. "That wasn't us," Bess said. "I'm sorry. Lots of people look like us."

Madame Curie pulled open a drawer and took out a black-and-white photo that was next to a small brown leather notebook. The photo was of a group of people, three adults and three children. They were all outside and wearing hats. The women were in long skirts, the children in shorts. The man next to Madame Curie had dark hair and a bushy mustache. "This photo was taken on that day in the Swiss Alps. You met all of us. Albert Einstein... his son. My two daughters and their governess..."

"What's a governess?" Bess asked.

"Someone who watches and teaches children," Madame Curie replied, handing Hazel the photo.

"Sorry," Bess said. "I would've remembered a governor."

Hazel sat down on one of the bar stools and looked at the picture closer, recognizing the man in the photo. "I would have remembered meeting Albert Einstein too. He's a very famous scientist."

Madame Curie took the photo back. "I suppose you would have remembered that." She picked up a glass tube and held it out in her hand, examining the liquid inside it. "I guess I was just hoping you really had traveled through time."

"We really have," Bess said.

Madame Curie laughed. "Maybe one day we will be able to jump into the future," she said. "If we can learn to be less curious about people and more curious about ideas."

Bess set her purse on the table next to a large gold coin sitting in an opened box. She reached for the coin, but Hazel shook her head at her sister.

"You heard the scientist," Bess said, picking up the box. "Be curious."

Hazel shook her head harder. "That doesn't mean touch everything. You didn't even ask."

Bess put the box with the coin back down, but Madame picked it up again and handed it to Bess. "One of my Nobel Prize medals," she said. "I had them out so I could donate them to the war effort. They said they needed everyone to donate their gold."

Hazel gasped.

"You must never be fearful of what you are doing when it is right," Madame said, half-smiling. "I'm not sure why they wouldn't take them."

Bess set the coin back on the table and reached in her bag, pulling out her small, plastic aquarium. "Froggestein needs to see this," she said. She took him out of his container and held him up to the coin. "That's a Nobel Prize," she explained to her frog as she picked it up and turned it over, showing it to Froggenstein. The coin was larger than any coin Hazel had ever seen before. One of the sides had a picture of a man with a beard, the other had a picture of two people. Hazel reached for the coin. She wanted to touch it too.

"Ribbbbbet," Froggenstein said. He wiggled in Bess's hands and she struggled to hold him. Suddenly, he jumped onto the stool, then onto a box and onto the floor.

Hazel looked at Madame Curie. Her eyebrows were in slants like her grandfather's eyebrows always were. She was not happy.

Froggenstein hopped across the room.

"Help me," Bess said to Hazel.

"Get him yourself, and hurry," Hazel replied. She did not want to help her sister catch her frog. She wanted to touch the

Nobel Prize like her sister had. It wasn't her fault Froggenstein was hopping all over the place. Like most everything, this mess was Bess's fault.

Bess ran after him, but he was very fast.

"He's heading to my main lab," Madame Curie said, pointing to the frog that was hopping toward a hall at the back of the room.

Oh no, not the main lab! That was the dangerous part.

Chapter Thirteen

Hazel looked from the medal to the frog hopping across the room and back at the medal again. She needed to work together with Bess, not play with an award. Froggenstein might break something or jump into something dangerous, or change history somehow.

She bit her lip and slid off her stool. "Okay, we'll corner him by the back hallway," she said. "Bess, go stand by the back, and I'll chase him over to you."

Bess rushed across the room so she was near the hall that led to the main laboratory. She stretched her hands and legs out, ready to catch her frog.

Hazel chased after Froggenstein. He hopped away from her, just like she wanted, but he jumped too high, landing right in the middle of a box on the floor. Glass rattled inside it, and Madame Curie groaned. "Please don't break anything. We are in the middle of a war. Replacing things will be difficult."

At least Froggenstein was trapped in the box. Hazel looked inside and laughed. One of the small glass jars had shifted onto his head. He was wearing it like a hat. She gently took the glass off of the frog while she tried to get up enough nerve to pick him up. He hopped out of the box before she got the chance, which she was kind of happy about because she did not want to touch frog germs.

Hazel chased Froggenstein back through the room, flapping her hands around wildly so he would change his course and hop over to Bess. It worked, but when Bess reached down to grab him, she missed and he hopped past her, down the hall toward the lab.

Hazel and Bess both raced to catch the frog, finally scooping him up in the middle of the hall.

"Okay," Bess said. "We should head home."

They had stopped right by a door with a glass window.

"Nice teamwork," Madame Curie said, walking toward them. She motioned to the door they were standing in front of, "This is my main lab. I took my radium to another city when the war broke out. But, I retrieved some of it when it seemed like things were safe so I could continue working with it. My husband and I worked together to discover this, part of the reason we won the Nobel Prize back in 1903. We were a pretty good team back then." She pressed her face against the window, like she was remembering. "This is radium."

In the darkness of the lab, they could see a faint bluish green glow coming up from a test tube on one of the tables in the next room.

"Whoa," Bess exclaimed. "It's beautiful."

"I always thought it looked like fairies," Madame Curie said, smiling.

"It does!" Bess yelled in agreement.

"Would you like to see it up close?" Madame asked. Her face seemed especially pale against her dark dress. "I don't usually let people into the main lab, but perhaps just for a minute."

Hazel and Bess both shook their heads no. "Our grandpa wouldn't like it," Bess said. Hazel hugged her.

Bess put her frog up to the window. "But Froggenstein has to see the radi-gum too."

"Radium," Madame Curie said. "Just be careful not to drop him again, like you dropped this." She held out the small brown leather notebook from the drawer where the photo of her and Albert Einstein was from. The notebook looked just like the one Hazel had in her back pocket. She put her hand in her pocket, but only felt hand sanitizer in there. It must've fallen out while she was chasing around

Froggenstein.

"You dropped this three years ago in the Swiss Alps. I kept it because the drawings and calculations were so interesting. It almost looked like two people had written the notebook, like they were arguing over designs and what it should be used for. What is the machine in the notebook..."

"We should get going... home," Hazel said instead of answering the scientist's question. She tried to remember how or when she could have dropped the notebook in the Swiss Alps, whatever that meant. She knew it was a place in Switzerland, but she'd never been there. "Thank you for finding my notebook."

The girls headed for the door.

"Let me just get my purse and Froggenstein's cage," Bess said.

"I'll get them for you," Hazel replied, running over to the back table where they still sat next to the Nobel Prize. "Teamwork," Hazel added.

"You just want to touch the Nobel Prize," Bess said, laughing so hard she snorted.

Hazel shrugged. "You're right," she said. It was only fair. Bess got to touch it earlier.

Hazel pulled the large coin out of its box and ran her finger over the pictures on it. It was heavier than she thought it'd be, and just as amazing. She put it back and raced out the door, still wondering how on earth she'd lost the notebook.

"I remember now," Madame Curie said as the girls ran from the room. "You told us you were returning a pair of glasses for your grandfather."

Hazel was running with Bess's purse, but she stopped when the scientist said that. She looked inside her sister's bag. No wonder Bess had wanted to drop the crank and leave. Hazel pulled out the thin wire glasses that used to be in the family's trunk.

Bess shrugged. "Teamwork," she said.

Chapter Fourteen

Hazel led the way, down the street and past the ladies still working on the x-ray equipment. "I cannot believe you took the glasses from the trunk. Now, we have to return them. We were supposed to decide on one thing. One thing, Bess. And we decided on the metal bar, remember?"

"We didn't decide that. You decided it. Working together means we both agree on a plan..."

Hazel thought about that for a second. Maybe she did have a tendency to take things over sometimes, but it was only because her plans were always better. She was older.

"It doesn't matter now," Hazel said. "We need to return the glasses and leave. We still have to clean our room before Bobby comes over. And we've already been here for hours."

"I liked it here," Bess said. "Good job picking the crank."

Hazel stopped herself from saying anything else. She smiled, looking off at the Eiffel Tower and the people walking around in long dresses and stiff suits. She looked over at the Radium Institute and the women learning about x-ray equipment. She thought about how she and her sister caught the frog and touched a Nobel Prize. She hugged Bess. "We do make a pretty good team," she said. "We'll decide together from now on. I promise I won't take over."

The time machine was right in the bushes where they left it. Bess lifted the dome lid and slid inside, placing the pair of glasses from her purse into the compartment under the control panel.

"At least we know who the glasses belong to," Hazel said.

"Who?" Bess replied. She turned her head to the side. Her eyes looked huge in her own glasses.

Hazel scooted in beside her sister. They closed the lid and hit the green button. The time machine rumbled to a start, shaking the ground around them. "Weren't you paying attention?" Hazel yelled over the sound of the engine. "We are about to see Madame Curie again, only this time she'll be with Albert Einstein. Remember? Three years before this."

"I guess we'll see," Bess said, twirling her finger by the side of her head, making a crazy sign. She hit the button with her other hand.

Blip. They were gone.

—

Hazel blinked her eyes open. The heat from the sun warmed her cheeks while the smell of flowers in full bloom tickled her nose. The dome to the time machine was already lifted and Bess was smiling at her, squinting in the thin wire glasses from before. "Ready?" she asked.

Hazel nodded.

The time machine had landed in a set of bushes again, like usual. The girls stepped out of it and walked over to a nearby trail, looking around in amazement. The soft sounds of summer filled the air. Birds chirped. Leaves rustled in the wind. They were on some sort of a mountain. Large rocks, meadows, and flowers surrounded them. A crystal blue lake was down below and in between the hills off in the distance, they could see a humungous rock mountain with snow at the top.

"It's beautiful," Hazel said.

"See?" Bess replied. "Choosing the pair of glasses was a good idea. Let's just stay here, and not play with Bobby." Bess was wearing her own glasses now. She put the other glasses in her purse with Froggenstein.

Hazel hugged her sister. She wanted to stay here too, but they had to get back.

The girls heard talking and laughing coming from up the trail. "Quick, let's hide and think of a plan," Hazel said, grabbing her sister at the last moment and yanking her into a clump of bushes. "I think Grandpa said something about remembering to tell the group that we were returning the glasses our grandfather borrowed. So let's wait until the group passes then we'll catch up and return them, quickly. We don't have much time. So we need to work together."

Hazel kicked her feet into the grass and dirt. *Was she taking over things again?*

"I mean, if you're okay with that. What do you think?" she asked her little sister.

"Good plan," Bess said as they high-fived.

"And remember," Hazel added. "That

we will be seeing Madame Curie three years before we saw her before. She won't know us."

"How are you so sure we're seeing her again, or that she won't know us?" Bess asked. "She'll know us."

"Just don't say anything. And remember, we can't take anything either, or leave anything, or change anything." Hazel reminded her sister. "So please, stick to the plan this time."

"I always do," Bess said, making Hazel nervous because if there was one thing she knew for sure. Bess never stuck to any plan.

Chapter Fifteen

Three children walked by the bushes they were hiding in, followed by a man with fluffy hair sticking out of his straw hat and a thick mustache, and two women in long dark dresses. It was just like the photo in Madame Curie's drawer. Hazel knew the older woman was Madame Curie and the man was Albert Einstein, along with their children and a governess.

Bess gasped and pointed when she saw the woman. "Madame Curie," she yelled, jumping out of the bushes. Hazel rolled her eyes. "So much for sticking to the plan," she thought.

The group stopped. They all turned and stared at the girls. Hazel had to admit she and Bess must have looked strange, two kids popping out of the bushes in the middle of nowhere, especially with one of them in a long sparkly movie-star dress.

The man finally chuckled. "Marie, your fans are coming out of the woodwork."

Everyone laughed and started to walk down the trail again.

Suddenly, Bess ran over and hugged the woman, almost knocking her over. "I didn't get to hug you good-bye before," Bess said.

"I'm sorry. Do I know you?" Madame Curie asked.

"Yes… we just met you like five minutes ago. You don't remember? I'm Bess and this is my sister, Hazel. You couldn't have forgotten us already. Remember, there was a war and no one was in Paris. And you were making x-ray cars to help doctors in battle..."

"A war?" The children said, gasping.

"I'm sure she's mistaken," Albert Einstein replied. "We would have heard about it in town."

Hazel pulled Bess aside and whispered. "Remember, Bess. That wasn't really five minutes ago. Madame Curie said she met two little girls who looked like us three years ago. Those two little girls were us."

Bess scrunched her face. "What?"

"It was 1916 five minutes ago. Let's check to see what year we've travelled to now," Hazel said.

Bess shook her head in disbelief. So Hazel took over. "Please, could you tell us what year this is and where we're at?"

Albert Einstein turned to the group. "And you all thought my physics questions were strange."

"It's 1913," Madame Curie replied. "And these are the Swiss Alps. Why are you asking? Are you feeling okay?"

It was just as Hazel thought. "See?" she said to Bess.

Bess pulled the pair of glasses from out of the bag. "I am so confused, but I guess these must belong to someone here," she said. "We're returning them for our grandfather."

Rrrrriiiiibbbbet!

Bess's sparkly purse jumped. She set the glasses down and opened her purse up. Froggestein suddenly sprung out of the bag and Bess gasped. "I guess I didn't close the cage right when we were in Madame

Curie's lab," she yelled as her frog hopped along the path.

Hazel rolled her eyes. *Not again.*

"Grab the frog," Bess yelled.

Soon, the whole group was following Froggenstein, but whenever someone bent down to scoop him up, he jumped away again. It was almost like he wanted to stay in the Swiss Alps of 1913, which Hazel could not blame him for at all. She wanted to stay here too and hike the trail with the mountains and lakes around it.

Froggenstein was just about to jump into a patch of overgrown flowers when Albert Einstein stopped him with the edge of his hiking boot. "This is your frog, I presume" he said, picking up the animal and handing him to Hazel. Hazel quickly handed him to Bess before the frog germs could get on her.

"Thank you, Mr. Einstein," Hazel said.

He smiled at Madame Curie. "It looks like you are not the only famous scientist around here," he said. "They know me too."

"Of course," Bess said. "You're very famous in the future where we're from."

Hazel rolled her eyes. *Why did her sister always say things like that?*

"Yes. And there was a war five minutes ago in Paris," one of the children said, making everyone laugh.

Albert Einstein bent down and picked the glasses up from the spot near her purse where Bess had left them. "My favorite pair of reading glasses. Thank you for returning them, even though I just lent them out no more than 20 minutes ago to a bearded gentleman who needed them. Actually, since you are such great fans of ours, you can keep them if you like."

He held his glasses out for Bess to take. And for the first time, Hazel didn't want her sister to stick to the plan. It would be nice to have a memory of meeting Albert Einstein and Marie Curie, and the glasses would be proof that they'd met the famous scientists.

Plus, it wasn't like they would be stealing them anymore. The scientist was giving it to them. But then, taking the glasses would go against the plan they had with their grandfather to work together to return the items to history.

Hazel looked at her sister. "Stick to the plan," she whispered.

"Okay, thanks," Bess said to Albert Einstein, swooping the glasses back from the famous scientist and putting them on.

Chapter Sixteen

The wind gently brushed through the leaves of the trees surrounding them and the soft smell of pollen filled the air. Hazel was just about to tell Bess she couldn't keep the glasses when Bess took the glasses back off and gave them to the famous scientist.

"No thank you," she said to Mr. Einstein. "I wish I could, but I promised to stick to the plan this time."

He took a step back. Hazel could tell he was surprised, and confused. Hazel was surprised, too. Maybe Bess really was learning how to work together.

The group said good-bye to the girls

and moved down the trail.

Hazel and Bess waited for them to get far enough away before they rushed back to the time machine.

"You stuck to the plan," Hazel said when they got to the bushes where the time machine was. "We're not taking anything with us from history. We're not leaving anything behind. We didn't change anything at all. I'm so proud of you."

"Why do you sound so surprised?" Bess said, raising the time machine lid and climbing inside.

Hazel laughed and got in behind her sister.

She knew by now how to operate the time machine a little more. In order to return to their spot in history, they only needed to place something from the farmhouse into the compartment under the control panel. She reached in her back pocket and pulled out the tiny bottle of hand sanitizer, placing it into the compartment.

Bess pushed the button, and the time machine rumbled on. But Hazel thought about the hand sanitizer and her back pocket. *The notebook hadn't been in her pocket! Where had she left it?*

She checked her other pocket as Bess pushed another button.

Blip. They were gone.

—

Hazel blinked her eyes, trying to force them to adjust to the dim lighting that surrounded her. She took a deep breath. The smell of damp attic filled her lungs.

Home. She looked around for her sister. Bess was by the door, and motioned for Hazel to come over there too.

"Mom's downstairs with Bobby," Bess said.

Hazel held in a gasp. "Mom's downstairs with Bobby? Oh no! Did she go looking for us?" Hazel said, remembering what Bobby had told them earlier. *If you don't open the door, I'm telling your mom to look for you.*

And none of their chores had been done!

Bess shushed her. "I don't know. They're wondering why they can't find us."

Hazel rolled her eyes. "Ugh. If they're wondering why they can't find us then that means they've been looking for us."

Bess shrugged. "Okay. What should we

do?"

Hazel stood frozen. She tried to think of a plan, but nothing came to her.

"Come on," Bess said, grabbing Hazel's hand and pulling her out of the attic door to the staircase. "We don't always need a plan. Let's just go."

Somehow Hazel knew not having a plan was probably the worst plan of all.

Chapter Seventeen

The girls rushed down the narrow staircase that led from the attic to the floor where their room was on. They almost crashed into their grandfather who must've been on his way up to the attic.

"Oh good." He grumbled. "There you are. Your mother's been looking for you."

Hazel's face dropped. "Sorry, Grandpa."

She thought she saw her grandfather smiling, but with such a thick beard she was never sure.

He put his hand on Hazel's shoulder. "Looks like you figured everything out okay. Just like I said, all you needed to do was work together."

He called down to the main floor. "Found them! They were playing hide-and-seek just like we thought."

Their grandfather winked at the girls then made his way up to the attic.

Hazel was sure her grandfather was crazy now. She and Bess hadn't figured anything out. They were supposed to have all their chores done before they did anything fun. And, they were about to be in huge trouble. Hazel also knew she needed to tell her grandfather that she not only looked through his old notebook, but that she also accidentally left it somewhere in history. She hoped she hadn't accidentally changed things by doing that.

Hazel trudged down the next set of stairs. Their mother was standing by the front door, arms crossed.

"I'm sending Bobby home," she said, opening the front door. "If you can't follow the rules then there is no play date."

Bobby stuck his tongue out at the girls from behind their mother's back. "I could always help them with their chores," he said.

Hazel's mother smiled at the freckle-faced boy. "That's very nice," she said. "But that wouldn't be right. We'll try it again another day."

Bobby went out the front door. "They're in trouble, though, right?"

Their mother didn't answer. "Good-bye, Bobby," she said, waving to their neighbor as he opened his umbrella and left into the rain.

As soon as the door was closed, their

mother turned to the girls. "I'm not happy, but I also realize why you did it."

Bess shrugged. "What do you mean?"

Their mother kissed both their heads. "You played first because I was the one who made those plans with Bobby. It wasn't fair for me not to ask you both what you thought about it."

Hazel and Bess hugged their mom. Her curls scratched their face as they squeezed her extra hard.

"Still, that doesn't mean you're not in trouble," she said when their hug was done. "There will be extra chores. Lots of them."

"We don't mind," Bess said, running up the stairs. Hazel ran after her, stopping to look up the stairwell that led to the attic. She wondered if their grandfather had anything to do with their mother's change of plans. He must have talked to her about it.

Hazel wanted to go up to the attic to see, maybe tell him about the strange notebook and ask him about the box full of pictures. She knew she needed to tell him about the notebook, at least. It must've belonged to both their grandparents and she wanted to know more about it. But it would all have to wait for another day. There was nothing she could do about it now.

"Come on. Let's go clean up the mess you made in our room," Bess said to Hazel as she opened their room door. "I mean that I made."

"No. You mean the mess we made," Hazel replied, then added. "Teamwork."

— The End —

Hi. Thank you so much for reading my book. I hope you liked reading it as much as I liked writing it. And if you did, please consider telling your friends about it and leaving a review.

Here are the other books in the Time Machine Girls series if you're interested:

Book One: Secrets
Book Two: Never Give Up
Book Three: Courage
Book Four: Teamwork

And if you'd like to know when new books are coming out, just have your parents sign up for my newsletter list on my website at www.ernestinetitojones.com.

Read on for more about Marie Curie.

Thanks again!
Ernestine Tito Jones

More About Marie Curie
And the Nobel Prizes

When I started researching Marie Curie, I didn't know much about her, except that she was a famous scientist who had been awarded two Nobel Prizes. But once I started reading her story, I couldn't stop. She was such an amazing person.

One of the first stories I read was the ingenious way she teamed up with her sister to get their degrees. At the time Marie was growing up in Poland, women were not allowed to study in universities. And Marie's family did not have much money for the girls to study in another country where women were allowed to earn degrees. But this didn't stop Marie. She made a deal with her older sister, Bronya, to work together. First, Marie would work as a tutor and set aside money to help Bronya pay for school in Paris. Then, Bronya would return the favor after she found employment with her degree.

With this plan in place, Bronya became a doctor and Marie became a scientist.

But this was just the beginning of Marie's amazing story. She and her husband, Pierre Curie, were both scientists who discovered radium and polonium by working together. And, Marie Curie dedicated her entire life to helping people through science.

What's true in the story?

Marie really did use her knowledge of radiation to create mobile x-ray cars in World War I called Petites Curies. She had to teach herself how to drive, how to do basic car repair, and how to set up and run x-ray equipment. She also had to convince people to donate their cars for the purpose

— and get the machine shop to turn them into vans. She was very good at teamwork and getting things done.

Marie really was friends with Albert Einstein too, and they vacationed together sometimes with her family and his. They really did visit the Swiss Alps together in the summer of 1913.

In the story, though, Madame Curie speaks English. If this were a real story, she would most likely have been speaking French or Polish.

Quotes in the Story Marie Curie Actually Said:

"Nothing in life is to be feared. It is only to be understood."

"You must never be fearful of what you are doing when it is right."

"Be less curious about people and more curious about ideas."

The Nobel Prizes
(An Explosive Idea)

The Nobel Prizes were started in 1900 by a man named Alfred Nobel who was famous at the time for being the inventor of dynamite. He became very rich off of that invention, but when his brother died, the newspaper mistakingly wrote that it was Alfred who had died, and the story was not a very good one. He realized people viewed explosives (his life's work) as harmful to society, and he wanted to change the way people saw him.

So, he decided he would help humanity with his fortune. When he died, he left a good part of his wealth to be used to give yearly prizes to people who did their best to help humanity. These prizes are given out in the fields of physics, chemistry, physiology or medicine, literature, and peace.

Marie Curie was the first woman to receive a Nobel Prize. She shared the Nobel Prize in Physics in 1903 with her husband, Pierre, and Henri Becquerel, the man who discovered radiation. She was awarded another Nobel Prize in 1911. This time in chemistry, making her the first person to win two Nobel Prizes. Her daughter Irene was also a Nobel Prize recipient. She won for chemistry in 1935.

Each Nobel Prize winner receives a gold medal, money, and a certificate. During the war when everyone was asked to donate gold items so they could be melted down, Marie Curie really did selflessly offer to donate her Nobel medals. They were refused.

Made in the USA
Middletown, DE
16 June 2021